D1462775

# My Pal, VICTOR

**Written by Diane Gonzales Bertrand**
**Illustrated by Robert L. Sweetland**

*For my pal, Kathleen M. Muldoon, who inspired this story.*

*—Diane*

*To my pal, Nancy.*

*—Bob*

★

Text ©2010 by Diane Gonzales Bertrand
Illustration ©2010 Robert L. Sweetland

Bertrand, Diane Gonzales.

My pal, Victor  / written by Diane Gonzales Bertrand; illustrated by Robert L. Sweetland;
—1st ed. —McHenry, IL : Raven Tree Press, 2010.

p.;cm.

SUMMARY: Two Latino boys experience carefree camaraderie.
Despite one boy's disability, fun and friendship
overpower physical  limitations.

English-only Edition
ISBN: 978-1-934960-84-4 hardcover

Bilingual Edition
ISBN: 978-0-9720192-9-3 hardcover
ISBN: 978-1-932748-72-7 paperback

Audience: pre-K to 3rd grade
Title available in English-only or bilingual English-Spanish editions

1. Friendship–Juvenile fiction. 2. Children with disabilities–Juvenile fiction.
3. [Friendship]. I. Illust. Sweetland, Robert. II. Title.

LCCN:  2003092133

Printed in Taiwan
10 9 8 7 6 5 4 3 2 1
First Edition

Raven Tree Press
A Division of Delta Systems Co., Inc.
www.raventreepress.com

**Free activities for this book are available at www.raventreepress.com**

PRINTED WITH
SOY INK

# My Pal, VICTOR

**Written by Diane Gonzales Bertrand**
**Illustrated by Robert L. Sweetland**

4

My pal, Victor, makes up great stories.

He points to a cloud and a dragon appears,

or a rocket ship, or the pyramids in Mexico.

Sometimes he includes us in his stories.

It's like a movie playing in our heads.

6

My pal, Victor, tells great jokes like, "Did you hear about
the chicken who wanted to dance the polka?"
Or, "Why did the elephant paint his toenails red?"

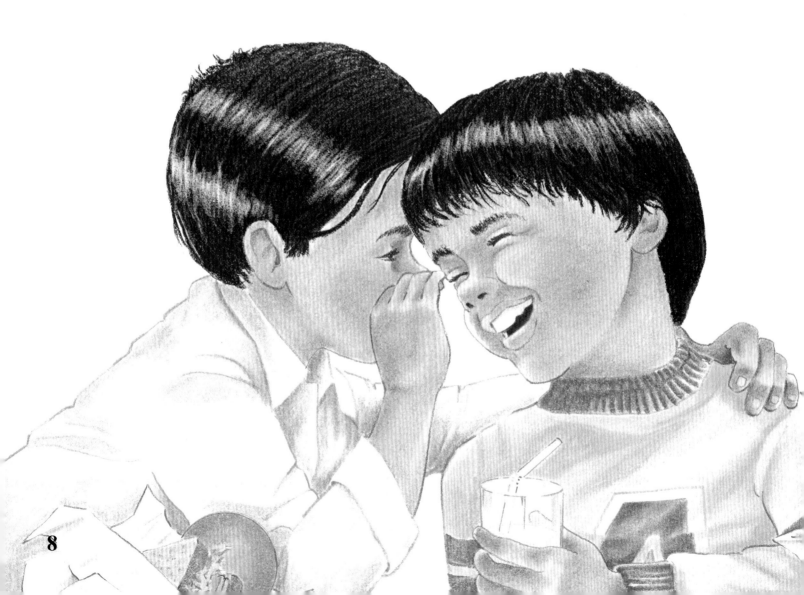

Or the one that goes:

"If you mix a parrot and a pickle together, what do you get?"

We laugh from joke to joke until our stomachs hurt.

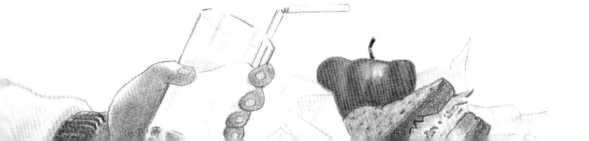

My pal, Victor, cheers loudest at my baseball games.

He claps and yells.

He whistles and shouts, "Go, Dominic, go!"

as I run around the bases.

**And he gives me a high–five when I make it home—SAFE!**

My pal, Victor, swims better than a fish.

We dive for pennies at the bottom of the pool.

He watches my famous fantastic belly flop.

I clap for his fabulous floating frog stroke.

My pal, Victor, whispers scary stories
at midnight when I sleep over.
He puts the flashlight under his chin.

19

He tells heart–booming stories about
ghosts and monsters and haunted houses.
Even my goose bumps get scared!

My pal, Victor, loves to ride the highest rollercoasters
and the dizziest, zoomiest, fastest rides he can find.

I walk out wobbly and dizzy,

but Victor points out the next ride we need to try.

My pal, Victor, throws a toy

for his dog to catch.

He blows big bubblegum bubbles.

He feeds the ducks his leftover lunch.

**My pal, Victor, and I do so many fun things.**

But, the most important thing about my pal, Victor,

is that he likes me just the way I am.

Answers to jokes found in this book are:
*page 8*    She couldn't find ballet shoes in her size.
*page 8*    So he could hide in the cherry tree.
*page 10*   A pickle who wants a cracker.